SO-AQM-817

Jack Kelly Simonson

discovers the ABC's on Sesame Street

With love from

Mommo and Poppo Ross

For A Special Little Boy

Story by
Lisa Ramée

Illustrations by
Frank Mayo

1996 Best Personalized Books, Inc.

4201 Airborn, Dallas, TX 75248

U.S. PATENTS 5,213,461 and 6,174,120 B1

© 1996 CTW. Sesame Street Muppets

**© 1996 Henson. Sesame Street and its
logo are trademarks/service marks of
CTW. All rights reserved.**

Jack Kelly Simonson, age 3 years, from Orange Park, Florida, was worried about his friend, Big Bird. He didn't look very happy. "What's wrong, Big Bird?" Jack asked.

"Today is Clean-Sweep Day, the day we all help clean up the neighborhood." Big Bird sighed. "It's going to be a lot of work."

"Don't worry," said Jack. "Sister Sami, Nana T. and Nana B. showed me you can make a big job easier by turning it into a game. Let's try it. We can pick up trash starting with each letter of the alphabet."

"That'll be fun!" Big Bird smiled. So Big Bird spread the word about the great idea Jack had and the Clean-Sweep game began.

"Look, someone left a broken airplane here, right next to a stack of beat-up boxes," Jack said. "Amazing, that's our A and B!"

"Hey, this box is full of empty cans," called Big Bird. "C is for cans!"

"Cool, we can recycle them," Jack said. "Wow, we have A, B, and C already! Now let's find something that starts with D."

Just then, Rosita joined them. "How about these dishes, Jack?" she asked, holding cracked dishes from her tea set. "You can have these too," she added, handing over a stack of old envelopes. "I took all the neat stamps off them."

"Excellent!" said Jack.

4

While collecting Elmo's gloves, Jack noticed a twisted water hose lying on the sidewalk.

"Watch out Big Bird!" he called. But it was too late. Poor Big Bird tripped on the hose and fell with a THUMP. Luckily, Big Bird's feathers padded his fall so he wasn't hurt.

Jack ran to help him up. "I'm glad you're not hurt, Big Bird. At least you found something that started with the letter H. This hose has so many holes in it, it must be trash!"

"How about using this to smooth your ruffled feathers, Bird?" snickered Oscar, handing Big Bird an old iron.

"Don't be silly, Oscar! But a rusty iron is ideal for our trash pile so we'll have an I!" Jack exclaimed.

"Boy, I don't know what we'll use for J," Jack wondered. "I sure wish Sister Sami, Nana T. and Nana B. were here to help."

"Me help, Jack," Cookie Monster said. "Jars with no cookies go into trash."

"Thanks, Cookie Monster! We'll put your jars in our recycling bin, instead of our trash pile," Jack said.

Zoe joined the group. "I found this in the park, Jack, but I don't know what it is."

"It's a kazoo, Zoe," Jack said. "But it's broken. See, it's cracked on the side. Let's add it to our trash collection, okay?"

"K," Zoe said with a smile. "Do you want these puzzle pieces I found too?"

"We're not ready for the letter P yet Zoe. We've found A, B, C, D, E, F, G, H, I, J, and K, so we're looking for L now," Jack explained. "We'll save your puzzle pieces for later."

"You know," Jack continued, "the park might be a good place to find more alphabet trash. Let's go!"

Jack was right. He and his friends picked up many things at the park to add to their collection.

They found a half-eaten lollipop in some litter on the ground. Someone had left a milk carton on a bench. They collected a net near a nest up in a tree, and even a broken oar by the pond.

"Now that we've got L, M, N, and O, we're ready for your puzzle pieces, Zoe," Jack said with a smile.

"P is for the puzzle pieces!" shouted Zoe.

"There's Ernie and Bert," Big Bird said. "Maybe they've come to help us clean."

"I hope so," Jack said. "We still haven't found anything for Q."

"We heard you were looking for trash," Bert said. "So Ernie and I cleaned out our closet."

"Let's see," Ernie said reaching into a large bag. "We have one queen from Bert's chess set. I lost the other pieces. There's my red rocket ship that broke last year. Oh, and here's an old skate."

"And here are some train tracks. Someone left them outside and they got trampled," Bert said. "Now you have Q, R, S, and T."

"Hey Jack," a grouchy voice called. "Take this umbrella. And here, Telly dropped off this vase. It's cracked...just like some people I know."

"Thanks Oscar, that's great for U and V," Jack said.

Just then Big Bird spied his wobbly wheelbarrow. "Wow, that's perfect for W. But Jack," Big Bird groaned, "What about X? There aren't any X-rays or xylophones around."

"X is tough. But look, Big Bird," Jack said with a smile. "Two of the umbrella's ribs are making an X. Can you see it?"

"Yes! And look, there's a tangled piece of yarn around one of the wheels of my old wheelbarrow!" Big Bird cried. "Yay! That's our Y!"

"Let's see. A, B, C, D, E, F, G, H, I, J, K, L, M, N, O, P, Q, R, S, T, U, V, W, X, Y, and Z." Jack sang.

"Oh no, Jack," Big Bird wailed. "We haven't found anything that starts with Z."

"Don't worry Big Bird," Jack said. "See, the zipper is broken on my old wallet. I had it in my pocket all the time."

"All right! Jack found Z!" Big Bird shouted. "We went through the whole alphabet, and we made the neighborhood look cleaner than ever."

"I sure had a lot of fun helping you with your big job, Big Bird. Now I'd better go home to Orange Park, Florida," Jack said. "Besides, I can't wait to tell Sister Sami, Nana T. and Nana B. how much fun it is playing games with the alphabet!"

Jack Kelly Simonson,

Enjoy this book.

A special gift from

Mommo and Poppo Ross

Manufactured by Best Personalized Books, Inc. Dallas Texas 75248